Collins

COPYCAT

CATHERINE MACPHAIL

CHAPTER 1

I blame everything that happened on my own good nature. I took her under my wing. She was plain and frumpy, and I said to my friend Indira, "Let's make Mimi our next project."

Big mistake.

You see, I used to be the most popular girl in the school – me, Chantelle Morgan – that is, until Mimi came along.

I can still remember the first day she walked into our class. Maybe "slouched" into the class would be a better word. She kept her eyes on the floor as if she was scared to look up at anyone, and Mr Barr, our teacher, said, "This is your new classmate, Mimi Ward. She's just moved into the new estate, and I want you to make her feel welcome."

Mr Barr's eyes swept around the classroom and rested on me. Which I thought was a bit of a cheek. I make everybody welcome. I'm a very nice girl. Ask anybody. Well, maybe not anybody … but ask my best friend, Indira.

"Now, take a seat over there, Mimi," Mr Barr said. "Beside Chantelle and Indira."

So Mimi starts to walk up to her desk. Well, not exactly "walk". Maybe "waddle" would be a better word. Then, she tripped over something – I think it might have been her own feet – and she fell flat on her face.

That Carrie Cox and her gang all started to laugh. And poor Mimi's face went brick red.

Well, I hate bullying of any kind, and I can't stand Carrie Cox. So I held out my hand to Mimi and I helped her to her feet.

Then I gave Cox one of my famous Chantelle glares. I was letting her know that from now on Mimi was under my wing, and she'd better not mess with her.

See what I mean about being nice!

Mimi was so grateful. She looked up at me and grinned. Unfortunately, she still had some bits of her breakfast cornflakes stuck in her teeth. Not a pretty sight. "Thank you very much," she said. Well, not exactly "said"; maybe "mumbled" would be a better word.

"It's my pleasure, Mimi," I said, and I flashed a smile at Mr Barr as if to say … see, I am making the new girl welcome, just like you asked. He didn't smile back.

I don't think he's forgiven me for coming to school with a white streak through my hair. I mean, it wasn't permanent or anything. It's just that I like to be different. That's why I wear the school uniform, my way, and my hair, my way. The Chantelle way. It's shoulder length, but I sweep it up at the back and backcomb it at the front. It's really different.

The first time I came into school with my hair like that, Mr Barr said he thought I'd had an electric shock. Cheeky so-and-so. That's another reason me and him don't get on.

But I was going to show him the kind of girl Chantelle Morgan was. I leaned across to Indira and I whispered. "This girl needs help, Indira. And we are the very girls to help her. She is going to be our project."

I was going to live to regret that.

At break we took her with us to the locker rooms. Halfway there she tripped. She ended up flat on her face again. "I'm sorry," she mumbled. "I'm so clumsy."

"No wonder you tripped, Mimi," I told her, trying to be helpful, as usual. "You never look where you're going."

She blushed again. "I don't like looking at people. They might notice me."

"Oh, and they don't notice you when you fall flat on your face?" I slipped my arm in hers. "Stand up straight, Mimi. Look ahead. You're friends with the two coolest girls in the school. You've got nothing to be ashamed of."

So what happens? Two minutes later she trips again and takes me down with her. Both of us, flat on our faces, and me, Chantelle Morgan, sprawled on the floor like a pancake. This girl definitely needed help.

Over the next few days me and Indira worked really hard trying to help her, but just getting Mimi to stand up straight was an effort. "I'm too tall," she kept saying.

"You're statuesque," I told her. "Or you will be when we've finished with you."

Finally, I went to the school library and took out half a dozen books. Mrs Sweet, the librarian, was well impressed. "I'm so glad you've started reading, Chantelle," she said.

I didn't have the heart to tell her I had no intention of reading any of the books. They were going in a pile on top of Mimi's head. I'd heard somewhere that's the way models learn to walk so that they stand up straight, and if it was good enough for them, it was good enough for Mimi.

"You're not leaving this locker room until you can walk straight without any of those books falling off," I told her.

For a while it was as if we were being attacked by books. Me and Indira had to leap about to avoid them. The books didn't just fall off her head; it was as if Mimi was firing them at us.

"I'll never walk straight, Chantelle," she kept saying.

"You'll stride about like a catwalk model when we've finished with you, Mimi," I told her.

And she smiled again. And, just for a second, that smile gave me the creeps. I don't know why … it was like a warning. Maybe I'm psychic or something.

CHAPTER 2

Helping people comes as second nature to me. I'm just that kind of person. When I was a little girl, I was always taking in stray puppies. They always ran away after a day or two though; I'll never know why. So I was determined for Mimi to make the most of herself.

"You could be pretty if you changed a few things," I told her.

"Like what?" Mimi asked.

"Well, like your hair … your face … your clothes … the way you walk … the way you talk … "

"That's not a few things. That's everything," she said, and she began chewing at her nails.

I pulled her hand away from her mouth. "And stop biting your nails. You could have lovely nails if you didn't bite them."

"Me?" and she held out her hands. She really did have lovely slim hands and long fingers, but her nails were bitten to the quick.

I looked at Indira. "She needs something fast. Something to stop her biting her nails while they're growing."

Mimi covered her hands as if I was about to put poison on them. As if I would ever do such a thing. Anyway, you can't get poison for that.

That night, Mimi and Indira came to my house and I fixed my French nails onto Mimi's fingers. They looked really natural, just as if they were real. They were a lovely oval shape, and after I'd put a glossy clear varnish on them, they looked fantastic. Mind you, I had to slap her hands away a couple of times to stop her biting them too.

"How can I ever thank you?" she mumbled again.

"Well, you could start by not mumbling all the time. Speak up, Mimi!" I told her.

"I never have anything worth saying," Mimi said in a whisper.

"Neither have I, but do you ever hear me mumbling? No! So take a lesson from me. Talk like me, and you'll find people will listen." I looked at Indira for support. "Isn't that true, Indira?"

She was laughing. "What? That you never have anything worth saying, or that people listen?"

I ignored that. "Lesson number two, Mimi. Speak out. Talk like me, Mimi, and you'll be okay!"

Mimi started to giggle. "You're so funny, Chantelle." She turned to Indira. "You're so lucky having her as your friend, Indira."

Indira was still laughing. "So she keeps telling me."

Even after just a few days I could see a difference in Mimi. She was walking straight, standing tall, and now she had those French nails she was using her hands more, waving them around as she spoke. She wasn't ashamed to show them.

"It's all thanks to you, Chantelle," Indira said. And I had to agree, it *was* all thanks to me. I think I've always been a role model, though I'm too modest to say that to anybody except Indira. Mr Barr told me once that when I do something, everyone else starts to copy it.

I don't think he meant it as a compliment though.

The teachers all complain about the way I wear my uniform. My skirt's too short, they say, and they moan at me because my shirt is always open at the neck and I always wear my tie hanging loose.

Actually, I think they're lucky I wear the uniform at all. I know a lot of schools where they don't bother. It's come as you please every day.

But you know, when Indira said that it was all thanks to me, it made me realise that helping Mimi to make the most of herself was actually making me feel better too.

Carrie Cox and her gang were always watching, smirking, waiting for something to go wrong. I tried to keep my eye on Mimi, but I couldn't watch her all the time, and one day I let Mimi out of my sight for five minutes.

Five minutes! I mean, I only went to the toilet, and when I came out, there were Carrie and her gang surrounding Mimi.

I could see Mimi going right back into her shell. Eyes down on the floor, shoulders bent, not saying a word back to them as they taunted her. She was just about to bite into my French nails when I leapt forward and grabbed Carrie by the arm. "Leave her be!"

"Get off me, Morgan!" Cox yelled. She tried to throw me off but I wouldn't let go.

Anyway, I could yell louder than she could. "I'm warning you, Cox, I'll make you very sorry …"

Suddenly, my favourite teacher Mr Barr pushed in between us. "What's going on here?"

"She just grabbed me, sir," Carrie said, in a little quiet voice. She sounded like a scared mouse. "Chantelle threatened me."

"Is this true, Chantelle?"

I so wanted to tell him the truth, that Carrie and her gang were picking on Mimi, but when I looked around all her pals had scarpered, and so had Mimi. It was just me and Carrie. And you don't grass, do you?

See what I mean about me being a nice person?

So I ended up on a report … again.

CHAPTER 3

Every second Friday, we have a disco at the school. Now I am a really nice person, no doubt about that, but as I told Indira, if Mimi came to the disco with us it would totally cramp our style, so I was hoping no one would tell Mimi about it.

I wasn't being selfish. Me? Selfish? As if. No. I was only thinking of her. I felt sure she wasn't ready to go anyway. She needed more time to build up her confidence.

I was just sneaking out of school on Friday afternoon, when Mimi caught up with me.

"What time does this disco start then?"

I was going to tell her it had been cancelled. The DJ had food poisoning. The hall had burnt down. But when I saw the hopeful look on her face, she reminded me of a puppy I once had when it used to beg for a treat. So what else could I do? What else could I say?

"Seven o'clock. I'll wait for you at the front door with Indira."

"You won't go in without me? I'll die if you're not outside."

"Of course we won't," I told her.

I was the one who nearly died when I saw her arrive. She was wearing a skirt that reached her ankles and an orange blouse with frills (yes, frills!), and she had her hair held back with pins, and even from a distance I could see what she'd had for her tea still stuck in her teeth. Broccoli.

"Nobody can be that ugly on purpose, Indira," I said in a whisper. I would never have said that out loud to Mimi, of course. It might have hurt her feelings, and I would never do a thing like that. There's not an unkind bone in my body.

I always walk into the disco with my head held high. Or maybe "swagger" would be a better word. I turn heads. I really do. Ask anybody. Well, maybe not anybody. But ask Indira. I did that night as well. I knew I looked good. Then Mimi stumbled in front of me and tripped me up, and I ended up sliding along the dance floor on my belly.

"Is this a new dance craze?" Carrie Cox laughed. "Don't think it'll catch on."

Mimi came rushing over and helped me up. As soon as I was on my feet, I felt dizzy. My nose started to bleed.

"I'm so sorry, Chantelle. All my fault. I am so clumsy."

"It's okay, Mimi, you couldn't help it." Well, that's what I said at the time. Now, I'm not so sure. After everything that has happened I wonder … did she trip me up on purpose?

That night at the disco was a total disaster. My nose wouldn't stop bleeding – it totally ruined my new white top – and my blood kept dripping onto the dance floor. Carrie Cox said I was a health and safety hazard. In the end I left early.

Next day, Mimi was on the phone, all apologies. "Has your nose stopped bleeding? I feel so guilty. It was all my fault."

She sounded so sincere that I began to feel sorry for her again.

"My mum's given me money to buy new clothes," she said. "Do you want to come shopping with me? You've got such good taste."

How could I refuse? She'd said the magic word that always makes me feel better.

Shopping.

And I suppose she was right: I have got really good taste. Ask anybody … well, maybe not anybody, but ask Indira. So off we went that afternoon, me, Indira and Mimi, into town to do some serious shopping.

"My mum always takes me to this shop," Mimi said when we got to the mall. "Bella Grande. It means beautiful."

I dragged her right past it. "It means BIG, Mimi. And you don't need BIG."

"What about this one?" She pointed at the Woollen Warehouse. "That's my mum's favourite. She gets all my cardigans there."

"It's a shop for old ladies, Mimi." I was beginning to think her mother didn't like her. I looked at Indira. "Lucky we're here, Indira. Let's show her where *we* shop."

So we spent the afternoon going round all our favourite shops. Mimi wasn't the only one looking for something to buy. I had money too. I almost bought this gorgeous red dress; I even tried it on. It looked fantastic. But it was scarlet red and far too short. I knew my mother would never let me go to the school disco wearing that.

"Anyway," I tried to make myself feel better. "I could never afford it."

With the money her mother had given her, Mimi got a new top, new trousers and new shoes. As we inspected her, all dressed up in her new clothes and wearing my French nails, Mimi looked almost human.

Except for her hair.

"You have to do something about that hair, Mimi," I said.

And she did.

CHAPTER 4

We were in the toilets, me and Indira, when we heard the commotion. At first I thought there had been a fight, and I planned to stay well away from anything like that. I was in enough trouble. But then we heard the "oohs" and the "aahs" and we knew there was something else going on.

Indira ran to the door and looked out into the corridor. The next minute she was oohing and aahing too. She looked back at me. "Oh Chantelle, you've got to see this!"

What I saw took my breath away. It was Mimi. She had taken it upon herself to have a haircut, and it made such a difference. It was swept up at the back, and backcombed at the front. Remind you of anything?

Yes. It was exactly like mine.

"You look fab, Mimi," somebody said.

"That hair makes such a difference, Mimi," someone else said.

It wasn't just her hair. It was the way she was standing, the way she was looking people straight in the eye, the confident way she was waving her hands about because she was still wearing my French nails! It was everything about her that made her look like ME!

"What's wrong, Chantelle?" Indira asked me when she saw me staring at Mimi, open mouthed.

"What's wrong? Look at her: her hair's cut exactly like mine!"

"But that's a compliment, Chantelle. Imitation is the sincerest form of flattery." And Indira hurried over to Mimi to tell her how pretty she looked.

I didn't feel flattered. Not one little bit. In fact, I had this awful feeling in the pit of my stomach, as if I had just downed a bowl of cold porridge in one go.

"I see your friend's got the same haircut as you, Chantelle." Cox had sidled up to me and before I could answer her, she added, "I think it suits her better actually."

And before I could grab her and rearrange *her* hair, she had moved off with her giggling pals.

That was the day things really began to change. Mimi still stuck with us, but she loved everyone's compliments, and she was always going off to talk to other people. "You don't mind, do you, Chantelle, about the hair?" she kept asking me. "It's just I love yours so much, and you did say I should do something about mine."

And of course, I had, hadn't I?

"Of course she doesn't mind, Mimi." Indira answered for me.

And through gritted teeth I agreed with that. "No, I don't mind, Mimi."

But I didn't really mean it. Because now, I felt Mimi was watching me all the time, studying me as if I was a science project. I would catch her looking at me out of the corner of her eye, and then she would look away quickly. It began to give me the creeps.

Indira couldn't understand why I was so bothered. "Oh come on, she admires you. She thinks you're fantastic."

Well, I couldn't fault her for that, could I? Maybe I was making too much of the whole thing. So, I decided to try to be happy for Mimi and her new hair.

But that all changed at the next school disco.

CHAPTER 5

So, there we were back at the school disco waiting for Mimi. I'd given her the same instructions that afternoon as we left school.

"We'll wait for you at the front door."

And once again she'd asked, in spite of all the compliments she'd been getting all week, "You won't go inside without me, will you? I'd die if I had to go in on my own."

And I'd warmed to her again. She still didn't have enough confidence to go into the disco on her own. Inside, she was still little timid Mimi.

Was it only two weeks ago I'd had a red face sliding along the dance floor with Mimi almost on top of me? Was it only two weeks ago I'd been standing beside her, embarrassed because she still had bits of her dinner stuck in her teeth? Was it only two weeks ago my nose had dripped blood all over the floor? It seemed more like months ago.

The rain was coming down in sheets that night, and it was blowing a gale, and Indira and I waited at the front door for ages for Mimi to arrive.

"We should just go inside; it's too wet," Indira said, shivering with cold.

"You go in, Indira, and I'll wait. She'll never have the courage to go in by herself. No point both of us getting soaked." (See what I mean? Nice person, I repeat!)

By the time she did arrive, my teeth were chattering, my hair was all over the place, and I'd stumbled and broken the heel off my shoe.

And then she arrived. She arrived like the Queen. Like a movie star at a Hollywood première. She stepped out of a taxi, with a big smile on her face. "My dad insisted I get one," she told me. "He said if I didn't, my hair would be all over the place in this rain and this wind … it would look a bit like … "

She looked at me, and blushed. She was about to say, a bit like mine! I limped into the disco in front of her. I stood at the mirror in the cloakroom to try and do something with my hair. The next thing I hear is all these gasps. I looked at my friends. They were all staring at something behind me, looks of pure amazement on all their faces. I swivelled round and guess what I saw?

Mimi, and what was she wearing? Only that fantastic red dress I had tried on, the one I almost bought, the one I knew would make my mum go spare if I tried to go out in it. And to make things worse … she looked better in it than I had!

Of course, Carrie couldn't keep her gob shut. "It must be like looking into a mirror, Chantelle. Except … this mirror really flatters you." Then she laughed like a hyena and so did all her friends.

"I hope you don't mind, Chantelle," Mimi said in her sweetest voice. "But you said you could never afford it and my mum treated me."

I had to bite my lip before I mumbled, "No. Not at all … "

But I did mind. Wouldn't you? My hair was standing on end like a toilet brush. The heel had come off my shoe, and somebody else was wearing the dress I'd really wanted, and she looked better in it than I had.

And that somebody was Mimi.

One of the boys even asked her up to dance. I watched her smiling and laughing, and now and again she'd flash me one of her innocent smiles.

Innocent? There was nothing innocent about Mimi.

Carrie Cox saw me watching her. "You're not jealous are you?"

Jealous? Me? There's not a jealous bone in my body.

But that night I had a bad feeling about Mimi. A feeling things were going to get worse.

CHAPTER 6

Mimi was changing. I could see it. Why couldn't anyone else? She was turning into me. Even Indira couldn't see it. "It's because she likes you," she kept telling me. "You're her hero."

"If she wants a hero, let her pick Batman," I told her.

But the Monday after the disco, Mimi came to school with her skirt above her knee, just the way I wore mine. She had the top button of her blouse undone, just like me. She wore her tie loose, just the way I did. And with her hair cut exactly like mine, from the back you couldn't tell the difference.

I tried not to let it bother me, but it did.

In the canteen that day I watched her walking up towards the table carrying a tray of food, and I was so tempted to trip her up. I longed for the days when she had tripped over everything.

She sat down across from me and the first thing she said was, "You've made my life so much better, Chantelle."

So then of course I felt guilty. I even managed a smile. "You made it better yourself, Mimi. I just gave you some good advice."

She reached across the table and squeezed my hand. "The best advice."

And for a day or two after that I really tried to think like Indira. Mimi was copying me because I was her hero. She wanted to be like me. She didn't mean any harm.

I kept thinking like that for just a day or two, until I heard her in the locker room.

Everyone had gone ahead to class, but I remembered I'd left my pencil case in my locker. I hurried back to get it and I was just about to push open the door when I heard the voice. A voice I recognised right away.

It was mine.

"I'm the nicest person in the school. Ask anybody ... well, maybe not anybody ... "

I opened the door just a little, and peered in. There was Mimi, standing in front of a mirror, and she was talking to herself ... in my voice.

What was she playing at?

"Hi! I'm Chantelle Morgan, and I'm wonderful." That was what she said!

I burst in the door and ran at her. "What do you think you're doing?"

And do you know what? She changed in front of my eyes. She became timid little Mimi again. "Oh, Chantelle, what do you mean?"

It all came out then. "I'm sick of you, Mimi, sick of you copying me. My hair, the way I wear my uniform, everything! I tried to help you and this is the thanks I get. You'd better stop this right now ... or else ... "

"Or else ... what, Chantelle?"

I turned round. Mrs Kay, the PE teacher, was at the door, glaring at me.

Mimi broke away from me and ran to her, as if she was scared of me. As if I was going to hurt her? Me, just about the nicest person in the school!

"Oh, Mrs Kay …" she said in her little Mimi voice. "I didn't mean any harm."

"So what exactly *were* you saying, Mimi, that has annoyed Chantelle so much?" Mrs Kay asked.

"I was just saying she was wonderful, Mrs Kay," Mimi said sweetly.

Mrs Kay stared at me. "Is this true, Chantelle? Did you hear Mimi say you were wonderful?"

And of course I had. I couldn't deny that. I tried to explain. "She was saying it in my voice, Mrs Kay. She was copying me, she was talking just like me … "

And suddenly it all sounded so stupid. She was copying me. So what? Why was I letting it bother me so much?

"It's a pity you don't know when someone is paying you a compliment, Chantelle."

Mimi reached out to me and I flinched away from her. "I'm so sorry, Chantelle, if I offended you … "

It was then I realised what a good actress Mimi was. She was certainly fooling Mrs Kay.

"Don't you apologise to her, Mimi. It's Chantelle who should be apologising to you."

And do you know what? That's what I had to do. To get out of that locker room I had to say sorry to Mimi!

Before lunch it was all round the school that I had threatened Mimi with grievous bodily harm. (And who told them that, I wonder? I'll give you three guesses.) People sneered at me in the corridors. They whispered about me in corners, and even Indira asked me, "You wouldn't really have hit her would you?"

And I had to be honest – after all, Indira is my best friend. "Well, I was thinking about it."

Of course, Indira only wanted to make me feel better, wanted to explain why Mimi was doing it. "So, she was trying to talk like you. Who was the one who told her she mumbles? Who was the one who told her to try and speak up, to talk the way you did?"

And I had, hadn't I? "Speak clearly," I had said. "Talk like me and you'll be okay!"

In that moment I knew I had created a monster.

I was Baron Frankenstein.

CHAPTER 7

I knew something was wrong as soon as I walked into school the next day. Carrie was waiting for me, face like thunder, hands on hips. I didn't know what her problem was, but she wasn't going to scare me. I swaggered right up to her, my Chantelle stare not leaving her for a minute.

"Have you got a problem, Carrie?"

"I thought it was you that had the problem," she said, and with that she whipped her phone out of her pocket and snapped on the voice message.

"Hey, Cox, it's me … Chantelle Morgan. I've had enough of you, Cox. When I see you tomorrow, you'll get what's coming to you."

When you're in shock, you can be really slow. I stared at the phone in her hand and then I stared at Carrie.

"Who is that?" and even as I asked it, I knew who it was.

It was me.

My voice.

"I didn't make that call," I said.

Carrie screwed her face into a sneer. "You're really trying to say that isn't you … even though your first words were 'it's me … Chantelle Morgan'. Do you think I'm stupid?"

I could have answered that, but I didn't want another fight. And anyway, I knew who it was.

"That's Mimi Ward, copying my voice. I heard her doing it yesterday!"

Carrie almost spat at me. "Mimi! What have you got against her?"

"You mean, what has *she* got against me!" I tried to snatch the phone from Carrie. She pulled her hand back and before I knew what was happening Carrie was on the floor, and I was on top of her and the phone was spinning across the tiled corridor, and my voice was on speaker.

"Hey, Cox, it's me … Chantelle Morgan. I've had enough of you, Cox …."

And the phone spun to a halt at Mr Barr's feet.

Could I convince them it wasn't me on that phone? Of course I couldn't. How could I hope to make them believe me?

I told them I'd heard Mimi talking in my voice the day before. I told them how good she was at impersonating me. I tried to make them understand. But they refused to believe that little Mimi could make such a nasty call.

"But I could?" I asked them. Me? She's not as nice as she tries to pretend, I told them. They could see the difference in her, couldn't they? They could see she was copying me.

But they had an answer for it all. Mimi admired me. She wanted to be like me. I should be pleased. I'd brought her out of her shell, they told me.

Trouble was, she'd invaded mine.

I thought at least Indira would believe me – and she said she did, but I could see she was only saying it to please me.

"You don't really think I made that phone call and can't remember!" I asked her.

"It can happen, Chantelle," she said. "I saw a film about it once. Maybe you had a blackout."

Just at that moment Mimi appeared round the corner. She took one look at me and turned on her heel. But I wasn't going to let her go.

Indira tried to stop me. "Leave her, Chantelle. You'll only get into more trouble."

But I couldn't leave it. I had to face her. I caught up with her outside the English class. Everyone was waiting to go in, but they stopped dead when they saw us. They were all eager to see what would happen. "Tell them!" I yelled at her. "Tell them it was you that made that call!"

She backed away from me as if she was scared.

"You made that call!" I shouted again. "Tell everybody it was you!" I wanted to hear her admit it.

And do you know what she did? She put her hand to her mouth as if she was ready to bite my French nails. I pulled her hand away. Then she mumbled in that whiny voice of hers.

"Oh Chantelle, please don't hurt me ...."

As if I would ever. As if I ever had.

"You're lucky I'm such a nice person, Mimi, or I might just do something awful to you." And I forced myself to turn away from her. But not before I added, "I'll prove you made that call. You see if I don't."

As I walked down that corridor, I could feel tears sting at my eyes. Me, Chantelle Morgan, crying! But who could blame me?

You should have seen the way the rest of the class, the school, were looking at me. As if they all believed Mimi!

I thought that was the worst moment in my life.

I was wrong.

After lunch, I stayed in the toilets long after the rest had gone on to class. I even told Indira to go ahead without me. I wanted to be alone for a moment. I sat on the bench and tried to think about what I could do.

Somewhere outside I heard the scream. I raced out of the toilets and ran to the top of the stairs that wound down to the atrium below.

There was Mimi. She was lying sprawled on the bottom step, clutching her ankle and crying. She looked up at me. "Chantelle!" She screamed it out.

And suddenly the corridor was alive with people, pouring out of classrooms or appearing from the rooms below and looking up at me from the atrium.

And those looks all said the same thing.

They thought I had pushed her.

CHAPTER 8

I wasn't expelled. I wasn't even excluded or given detention. They couldn't do anything to me because, you see, Mimi refused to say it was me who pushed her.

"I don't know what happened, sir," she told Mr Barr when he asked her. "Maybe I just tripped. I'm so clumsy." But when she said it her eyes glanced across at me and then looked away quickly, as if she was afraid of me. Can you believe that?

So, in spite of not actually being accused, I was still given a lecture and a warning.

"Anything happens to Mimi, Chantelle," Mr Barr said, "and you'll be the prime suspect."

The school might not have excluded me, but I felt as if I had been excluded by my classmates. They had all heard me say I might do something awful to Mimi.

Now they all believed I had. They turned away from me as I passed them. They only spoke to me when they had to.

So, here I was, watching Mimi, surrounded by my friends, looking exactly like me, right down to my French nails.

It was like watching my evil twin.

Even Indira, my very best friend, couldn't see what she was doing. "She still might not have meant any harm, Chantelle. I mean, she didn't tell anybody you pushed her down the stairs, did she? She could have lied, got you into a lot of trouble, and she didn't. Everybody would have believed her." Then she added quickly, "Except me, of course."

I wished Indira at least would understand. "What she did was worse, Indira," I told her. "She made people think she wasn't saying because she was so scared of me. Me, Indira! When have I ever scared anybody?"

Indira bit her lip. "Well, there was that boy, remember ... he used to run a mile whenever he saw you."

"Oh him! I wouldn't really have cut his hair ... they weren't even real scissors!" I let out a big long sigh. "I'm so depressed about this, Indira."

Indira tried to make me feel better. "Look at it this way, Chantelle. You've done a wonderful thing. You took an ugly duckling and turned her into a swan."

But I had an answer to that. "I didn't turn her into a swan ... I turned her into a vulture."

I was really down for a couple of days. I left school on Friday and didn't want to do anything or go anywhere. Mum and Dad wanted to know what was wrong with me. I was usually so cheery and happy, especially on a Friday when I was looking forward to the weekend. Instead, I moped in my bedroom.

My mum finally came up to my room.

"Are you going to tell me what's wrong? Have you fallen out with Indira?"

As if!

"No, of course not."

"You're not being bullied, are you?"

In a way I was. Mimi was making me almost afraid to go to school. But I couldn't tell my mum the truth. It all sounded so silly when I said it aloud.

She sat with me for ages trying to find out what was wrong. "I'll be fine in a couple of days. I promise. Don't worry about me."

She gave me a big hug. "No wonder I'm worried. This isn't like you, Chantelle, this isn't like you at all." When I was alone again Mum's words kept pounding in my ears. "This isn't like you, Chantelle. This isn't like you, Chantelle."

No, I kept thinking, how could I be "like me", when it was Mimi who was like me now.

She had copied my hair, my clothes, the way I walked, the way I talked. She had copied everything about me. She had taken me over, piece by piece.

That's when it hit me like a brick in the face. I had the answer! I knew what I was going to do. I knew how I was going to beat Mimi. And I was going to beat her at her own game.

CHAPTER 9

I walked into school on Monday, and you could see every eye on me. Mouths open, eyes wide, not believing what they were seeing. Mr Barr dropped all his papers; they fluttered like butterflies down the stairs.

"Chantelle! What have you done to yourself?"

I grinned. "I've done exactly what you've always told me to do, sir."

And I had. I'd had my hair styled and now it was no longer in untidy spikes. It lay on my shoulders, bouncy and shining. I was wearing my school skirt exactly as it was meant to be worn, just below the knee, regulation length. My shirt was tucked in and buttoned up to the neck, and my tie was firmly in place the way Mr Barr was always asking me to wear it. I looked like the perfect schoolgirl.

Mr Barr could hardly speak. He was well impressed. "Chantelle. I always knew you could look smart if you put your mind to it."

I think I had made his day.

And then I saw Mimi. She was standing with her back to me, looking exactly like me, or how I used to look, surrounded by her/my friends. They saw me first. Their mouths all opened so wide they looked like a shoal of fish, and Mimi slowly turned round to see what they were looking at. I gave her such a sweet smile as I swept past her. Mimi didn't smile back. Her eyes were like slits and her mouth was shut tight, her lips pressed together as if a cloud of venom would burst out if she dared to open them.

Timid little Mimi, innocent little Mimi, she knew exactly what I was doing.

"Well, look at you," Carrie Cox sneered when she saw me. "Who is little Miss Perfect?"

"Eat your heart out, Cox," I said, as I walked past.

I caught sight of someone in the glass as I strode up the corridor towards the classroom. A girl was walking confidently toward me. She was wearing the uniform exactly as it was meant to be worn. Her hair was shiny and bounced on her shoulders. Her face was fresh and bright. It was a girl I had never seen before, and it was me! How funny is that!

Everyone commented on it. The teachers raved about it.

"What a difference, Chantelle."

"You look wonderful!"

"You don't look like the same girl!"

Even the other girls were impressed. "Where did you get your hair cut like that?"

"It makes you look like a different person."

And that, of course, was the idea.

I watched as Mimi simmered. She didn't look a bit like me anymore, and I could tell she didn't like that. I saw her all that day, watching me. She wouldn't let this go. Not a girl who had pretended to fall and make out that I had pushed her. No, not Mimi.

Something was coming, but I didn't know what. So I was watching Mimi as closely as she was watching me.

I was just about to go into Maths when I heard the rest of my class already inside, talking. And they were talking about me.

"What do you think Chantelle's playing at?" someone was saying. It sounded like Carrie. "All dressed up in her uniform?"

"But she did look good, Carrie," someone else said. "Everyone says so."

"Well, that's it, isn't it? She's just looking for attention." And I knew that *was* Carrie Cox.

And then, another voice broke in, and I recognised that voice too.

It was mine.

"Hello! I'm Chantelle Morgan, and I want everybody to look at me ... or else!"

There was a stunned silence. I pushed open the door just a little and peeked into the classroom. Everyone had turned their attention to Mimi. For a split second she didn't realise what she'd done, but as soon as she did, her face went bright red and her hands flew to cover her mouth as if she wanted to stuff the words back in.

It usually takes Carrie a long time to figure things out. She was quick this time. She turned right round to Mimi. "That's the voice I heard on my phone! It *was* you that phoned me!" Carrie said.

Mimi was shaking her head. "No ... no ... honest."

"Chantelle wasn't telling lies. You can mimic her. You sounded just like her."

"No, no …" cried Mimi. "I don't know how I did that; I've never done it before."

Carrie reached out to grab her, but one of her pals held her back.

"Bet she didn't shove you down the stairs either," Carrie said.

Mimi mumbled. "She did. Yes, she did."

"You're evil, Mimi," Carrie said. And they all moved away from Mimi as if they might catch something from her.

And that was when I made my entrance. I pushed the door wide and walked in without looking at any of them. I ignored them all. I sat at my desk and I took out my books and I said nothing. Inside, however, I felt great.

Mimi had given herself away, big time. She had so wanted to stay in the limelight that she had made her big mistake. And I had had nothing to do with it.

And that really was the end of Mimi. She didn't last long as me. My French nails fell off and she started biting the old ones again, and without me to copy she forgot how to do her hair. It grew and lay in long lank strands on her shoulders.

This time I didn't offer to help her. Nobody did. They were all too scared. Nicest person in the school, me, yes ... but I can only go so far.

And me? Did I change back to old Chantelle?

No. I didn't. I liked the way I looked now, and you know what? Everyone else started wearing their uniforms exactly like me. You see, Mr Barr's right. People want to be like me. I suppose I am a sort of a role model, though I would never say that to anyone. I'm far too modest. Ask anybody ...

But in a way, Mimi taught me something too. I'm still the coolest girl in the school because I know now that coolness comes from within. It doesn't matter what you look like on the outside, it's what's inside that matters.

In fact, I sometimes wonder, *who* gave *who* the makeover?

Reader challenge

Word hunt

 On page 18, find a verb that means "jeered at".

2 On page 26, find an adjective that means "straightforward and honest".

3 On page 63, find a verb that means "sulked".

Story sense

4 Why did Chantelle decide to make Mimi her "next project"? (page 2)

5 Why does Indira laugh at what Chantelle is saying? (page 14)

 Why does Mrs Kay believe Mimi is paying Chantelle a compliment? (page 47)

7 Why did Mr Barr say Chantelle would be the prime suspect if anything happened to Mimi? What made him think this way? (page 60)

 Chantelle claims she was the most popular girl in the school. Do you think she was really that popular? Give reasons.

Your views

9 At what point in the story did you realise Mimi was mimicking Chantelle?

10 Did your opinion of Chantelle or Mimi change during the story? Give reasons.

Spell it

With a partner, look at these words and then cover them up.

- confident
- permanent
- innocent

- confidence
- permanence
- innocence

Take it in turns for one of you to read the words aloud. The other person has to try and spell each word. Check your answers, then swap over.

Try it

With a partner, re-enact the scene on pages 44 to 46 where Chantelle catches Mimi mimicking her in the mirror. Think about how Mimi's body language and facial expressions would change when Chantelle walks into the room.

William Collins's dream of knowledge for all began with the publication of his first book in 1819. A self-educated mill worker, he not only enriched millions of lives, but also founded a flourishing publishing house. Today, staying true to this spirit, Collins books are packed with inspiration, innovation and practical expertise. They place you at the centre of a world of possibility and give you exactly what you need to explore it.

Collins. Freedom to teach.

Published by Collins Education
An imprint of HarperCollins*Publishers*
77-85 Fulham Palace Road
Hammersmith
London
W6 8JB

Browse the complete Collins Education catalogue at **www.collins.co.uk**

Series consultants: Alan Gibbons and Natalie Packer

10 9 8 7 6 5 4 3 2 1
ISBN 978-0-00-754622-0

British Library Cataloguing in Publication Data.
A catalogue record for this publication is available from the British Library.

Commissioned by Catherine Martin
Edited by Sue Chapple
Project-managed by Lucy Hobbs and Caroline Green
Production by Emma Roberts
Illustration management by Tim Satterthwaite
Typeset by Jouve India, Ltd
Cover design by Paul Manning

Acknowledgements

The publishers would like to thank the students and teachers of the following schools for their help in trialling the *Read On* series:

Park View Academy, London
Queensbury School, Bradford
Southfields Academy, London
St Mary's College, Hull
Westergate Community School, Chichester